FOREVER

POST CARD

CENT

USA

19¢

2¢

5¢

8¢

AIRMAIL

USA

55¢

$1.00

29 CENTS

To the real Arfy

Visit us on the Web! rhcbooks.com

Educators and librarians, for a variety of teaching tools, visit us at RHTeachersLibrarians.com

Library of Congress Cataloging-in-Publication Data
Name: Cummings, Troy, author.
Title: Can I be your dog? / Troy Cummings.
Description: First edition. | New York : Random House, [2018] |
Summary: A dog looking for a home sends letters to prospective owners on Butternut Street, with surprising results. |
Description based on print version record and CIP data provided by publisher; resource not viewed.
Identifiers: LCCN 2015043998 (print) | LCCN 2016020399 (ebook) |
ISBN 978-0-399-55452-0 (hardcover) | ISBN 978-0-399-55453-7 (lib. bdg.) | ISBN 978-0-399-55454-4 (ebook)
Subjects: | CYAC: Dogs—Fiction. | Letters—Fiction.
Classification: LCC PZ7.C91494 (ebook) | LCC PZ7.C91494 Can 2017 (print) |
DDC [E]—dc23

MANUFACTURED IN CHINA

10 9 8 7 6 5 4 3

First Edition

CAN I BE YOUR DOG?

TROY CUMMINGS

Random House 🏠 New York

DEAR PEOPLE AT YELLOW HOUSE,

WOOF!!!

CAN I BE YOUR DOG?

I AM POTTY TRAINED, AND I HAVE MY OWN SQUEAKY BONE.  ALSO: I LOVE TO PLAY!

I SEE YOU HAVE A CAT, BUT I'M WILLING TO WORK WITH YOU.

WHOOOOOOO'S A GOOD DOG? I AM!!

SINCERELY,
ARFY

P.S. I KNOW EVERY HOUSE ON BUTTERNUT STREET, BUT I ASKED YOU FIRST!

Dear Arfy,

We're so sorry, but you cannot be our dog.
Our cat is, um, allergic to dogs.

Good luck in your search!

The Honeywells

Look, pal.

I've got a bone to pick with you. Last time I let a dog into my shop, a dozen meatballs went missing! Sorry, but there's NO WAY I'm taking in a pooch.

Veronica Shank
BUTCHER

P.S. No hard feelings. Enjoy these dried giblets, and good luck finding a home.

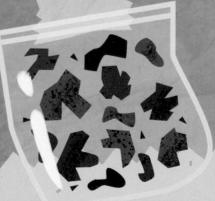

NOM
NOM
NOM

DEAR FIRE STATION NO. 5,

CAN I BE YOUR DOG?

I CAN FETCH YOUR BOOTS! PLUS, LET'S JUST SAY I KNOW MY WAY AROUND A FIRE HYDRANT. I'VE SNIFFED OUT EVERY SINGLE ONE ON BUTTERNUT STREET. (AND YOURS IS THE SHINIEST!)

-ARFY

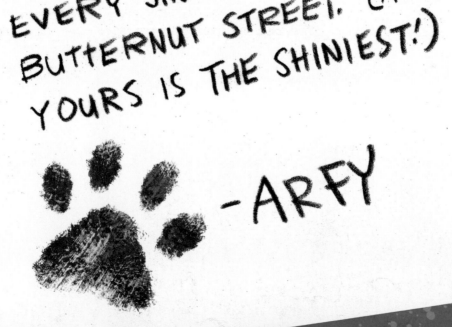

BUTTERNUT STREET
FIRE STATION

Dear **APPLICANT**:

Thank you for your interest in working with the

BUTTERNUT STREET FIRE STATION.

Unfortunately, the position of:

FIRE DOG

has already been filled.

We will keep your letter on file. Best wishes
in your search.

Station No. 5

DEAR JUNKYARD GUY,

I'M NOT GONNA LIE.
YOU'RE MY NEXT-TO-LAST CHOICE.
BUT THESE PAST FEW DAYS
HAVE BEEN ROUGH.

ROUGH! ROUGH!
RRRRRRR-ROUGH!

SO, PLEASE, CAN I BE YOUR DOG? I DON'T
EAT MUCH, AND I CAN BARK IF PEOPLE
TRY TO STEAL YOUR JUNK AND STUFF.

HOPEFULLY YOURS,

ARFY

DEAR LAST HOUSE
ON BUTTERNUT STREET,

CAN I BE YOUR DOG? I SEE THAT
YOUR YARD IS FULL OF WEEDS,
AND YOUR WINDOWS ARE BROKEN.
AND THERE'S A FUNNY SMELL.

BUT I'M NOT PICKY.

JUST LONELY.

-ARFY

ARFY
SOGGY BOX
IN THE ALLEY
BUTTERNUT ST. POST OFFICE
RETURN TO SENDER
NOBODY AT THIS ADDRESS!
LAST HOUSE ON
BUTTERNUT STREET

Dear Arfy,
Can I be your person?

I need a friend who will be with me no matter what: snow, rain, heat, or gloom of night.

And I see that you already know everyone on Butternut Street!

I know you'll make a first-class partner.

With hugs and head scratches,
Mitzy Whipple
Letter Carrier

P.S. If you agree, meet me at the big blue mailbox.

DEAR MITZY,
YOU KNOW WHAT?
MY TAIL HAS BEEN WAGGING
EVER SINCE I GOT YOUR NOTE.
MY ANSWER IS: YES!!
TRULY YOURS,
-ARFY
P.S. WOOF!

Here's how **YOU** can help a homeless animal:

ADOPT a shelter animal instead of buying a pet.

VOLUNTEER at a shelter or a pet adoption event.

SPAY OR NEUTER YOUR PET so there will be fewer fur babies to find a home for.

DONATE to your local animal shelter or a national animal-advocacy group, such as:

* American Society for the Prevention of Cruelty to Animals (aspca.org)
* The Humane Society (humanesociety.org)

Extend a helpful paw so all our animal friends can find forever homes!

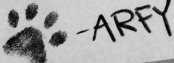 —ARFY